DRAGONS
father and son

To Maddalena and Giovanni
A. L.

For Yves Badel
R. B.

Quarto is the authority on a wide range of topics.

Quarto educates, entertains and enriches the lives of
our readers—enthusiasts and lovers of hands-on living.

www.quartoknows.com

© 2017 Quarto Publishing plc
Text © Alexandre Lacroix
Illustration © Ronan Badel
Translated by Vanessa Miéville

First published in paperback in 2018 by
words & pictures, an imprint of The Quarto Group.
The Old Brewery, 6 Blundell Street,
London N7 9BH, United Kingdom.
T (0)20 7700 6700 F (0)20 7700 8066
www.QuartoKnows.com

A catalogue record for this book is available from the British Library.

ISBN 978 1 78603 351 2

Manufactured in Guangdong, China TT052018

9 8 7 6 5 4 3 2 1

DRAGONS
father and son

Written by
Alexandre Lacroix

Illustrated by
Ronan Badel

words & pictures

Once upon a time, there was a little dragon called Drake. He lived with his father in a cave at the bottom of a steep-sided valley.

One day, Drake's father told him, "Listen, son, you're a big boy now. It's time you behaved like a real dragon. Tomorrow, you will go to the village on the other side of the mountains, where you will burn a few houses."

"But why?" asked Drake.

"It's tradition!" rumbled his dad.
"Do you want to be a dragon or not?"

That night, Drake struggled to sleep, tossing and turning in the straw of his cave. He had hardly ever breathed fire, and only to grill himself a small slug or caterpillar as a snack. But burn a house? No way!

The following morning, Drake flew off
to the village where the humans lived.
He spotted a little house on its own,
with walls made of wood.

"This will make a fine blaze!" he thought.

But just as he was taking a deep, deep
breath to set the fragile building alight,
Drake saw a little boy appear through
the front door.

"Wow! A dragon!" the child cried out.

"Aren't you scared of me?" Drake asked.

"No way! I've never seen a dragon before!
I'm pleased to see you really do exist."

"But you do realise I was about
to set your house on fire?"

"Burn down my house? Why?"

"My dad calls it tradition."

"Hmmm. I see. And if you don't do
what he says, will you be told off?"

Drake nodded.

The little boy thought for a moment,
then announced, "I have an idea. If you
want a big blaze, I know just the place."

The little boy led Drake to a square
building in the centre of the village.

"There you go!" he said. "You can set
these old walls on fire!"

"But what is this place?"

"This is my school," answered the boy,
a little sheepishly. "I haven't done my
homework. If you burn the school down,
I'll owe you a favour."

"I see," said the dragon, who had
never been to school and was not
sure he fully understood.

Once again, Drake took a deep, deep breath. Smoke was already coming out of his nostrils, when a woman appeared on the front steps. It was the teacher.

"Wait, young dragon! You can't do that!" she cried.

"And why not?"

"Because the children who come here every day are your biggest admirers," she answered mischievously. "I read to them about the legends of your renowned ancestors and they really loved it. They also like to draw dragons. Stay there, I will show you..."

The teacher came back a moment later with a large drawing.

"Do you like it?" she asked. "Please, take it. It's a gift."

On the drawing, Drake saw a majestic dragon, as red as a tomato, with a neck in the shape of an S, and teeth as sharp as an axe.

"Thank you, that's very kind, but I am on a mission," the little dragon explained. "Yesterday, my dad asked me to burn a house down."

The teacher thought about this and said, "Why don't you go to the riverside? There's an abandoned shack there which could do the trick."

By the river, Drake did find a shack, sheltered beside a huge rock. For the third time that day, he took a deep, deep breath. He was about to produce a huge spray of fire, when an old man, sitting nearby on the bank, put his fishing rod down and spoke to him.

"Ah, you couldn't have come at a better time," the old man told him. "You see, I caught twelve magnificent trouts, but I haven't got a single match. If you help me cook my lunch, I promise you a feast that you won't forget."

"Why not?" agreed Drake, who was a little hungry.

The fisherman, who kept a few things
in the old shack, went inside to look for
a bag of coal and a barbecue on wheels.
Drake blew over the coal, sparking long
flames which roasted the fish. With their
feet soaking in the river, they enjoyed
a delicious meal.

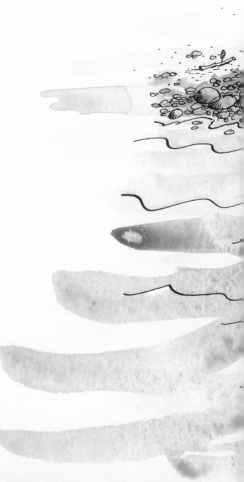

When Drake flew home, the little dragon's father was waiting impatiently for him.

"So, tell me everything, Drake. What did you do? I hope that you burned down the village!"

"Well, as it happens, I didn't burn down a single house."

"Why not?" cried his father.

"Because I didn't want to upset the villagers. They were all really kind to me!"

Hearing this, Drake's father exploded with anger. "What is this? Making friends with humans! What's going to become of us if they no longer fear us? They're ferocious creatures!"

"No, dad, you're wrong!
Look at the gift they gave me."

And Drake showed him the drawing.

"What is it?"

"It's a portrait of you, of course! You're their
biggest hero!" said Drake, who had learned a
lot from the humans about being smart.

Drake's father had to admit, the portrait was quite magnificent. Across his face, a small, proud smile appeared. Perhaps it was better to be admired than feared, after all.